TO THE LIMIT

WHITEOUT

VANESSA LANANG

darbycreek
MINNEAPOLIS

Darby Creek
A division of Lerner Publishing Group, Inc.
241 First Avenue North
Minneapolis, MN 55401 USA

For reading levels and more information, look up this title at
www.lernerbooks.com.

Cover and interior images: railway fx/Shutterstock.com (snow texture); Vadim Zakharishchev/Shutterstock.com (snowboarder).

Main body text set in Janson Text LT Std.
Typeface provided by Adobe Systems.

Library of Congress Cataloging-in-Publication Data

Names: Lanang, Vanessa, author.
Title: Whiteout / Vanessa Lanang.
Description: Minneapolis : Darby Creek, [2019] | Series: To the limit | Summary: Hoping to be a professional snowboarder like her father, sixteen-year-old Jessa Castillo ignores an approaching storm to practice snowboarding with her brother, Pax, fourteen, but soon the two are trapped in a blizzard.
Identifiers: LCCN 2018023428 (print) | LCCN 2018030151 (ebook) | ISBN 9781541542006 (eb pdf) | ISBN 9781541540378 (lb : alk. paper) | ISBN 9781541545564 (pb : alk. paper)
Subjects: | CYAC: Snowboarding—Fiction. | Brothers and sisters—Fiction. | Blizzards—Fiction. | Survival—Fiction. | Hispanic Americans—Fiction. | Family life—Fiction.
Classification: LCC PZ7.1.L27 (ebook) | LCC PZ7.1.L27 Whi 2019 (print) | DDC [Fic]—dc23

LC record available at https://lccn.loc.gov/2018023428

Manufactured in the United States of America
1-45242-36624-9/24/2018

For my girls, Sophie and Frankie—
don't ever let a storm keep you
from your dreams.

CHAPTER 1

Don't wipe out. Don't wipe out.

Not the best mantra when you're halfway down the ramp and headed into the first section of a slopestyle course. I ignored the you're-not-good-enough voice in the back of my head and crouched lower on my snowboard. *Nope, I'm not going to listen. Not this time,* I thought as I picked up speed. *I can do this.*

With my route planned out for the course, I hit the first rail section with ease, my board sliding across the metal bar backward. I spun off the end of the rail so I was facing forward into the next rail section.

I had a few tricks in my wheelhouse, but I had to decide which ones would impress the judges the most. *Think fast, Jessa.* Two tricks were possible, but the real question was if I could hit three.

I imagined the cheer of spectators along the course and focused on my spins, hitting two one-eighties off the last two rail sections. I couldn't play it safe on the jumps. *It's all about big air*, I reminded myself.

Out of the first jump I stomped a full three-sixty rotation, and off the second one I managed to add a board grab. Now came the final jump—I needed to land this backside five-forty. Unlike my first jump, this one added another one-eighty rotation, and landing backside meant I'd hit the ground before I saw it. I rode up the ramp in a straight line, and as I got to the lip of it, I threw my arms and popped my back foot to get enough momentum for my spin. I pulled my legs up to my body, and when I reached the maximum height in the air, I was right where I needed to be. In my head, I could hear the click of cameras from every snowboarding magazine covering the event.

Coming into my landing, I extended my front leg so the nose of my board would hit the snow first. *Yeah, I got this,* I thought before I hit the landing harder than I wanted to and steadied myself with a hand to the ground. It'd be a deduction for not sticking a perfect landing, but I imagined cheers from the crowd saying it was my best run yet.

I skidded to a stop, pulling my goggles up, and unclipping one of my boots from my snowboard. If I could repeat that run at next week's competition, I wouldn't need the extra practice on that backside five-forty. A girl could dream. But at least I didn't wipe out.

I shaded my eyes with my hand and peered up at the mountain, the snow-capped peaks fading into the pale blue sky. *The air is fresher up here. The world is brighter up here. And the . . .*

Out of nowhere, a rider came dangerously close to crashing into me. He tumbled into the snow right at my feet and then laid out on his back, limbs spread out like a star. I shook my head. Some of these snowboarders needed babysitters, especially this one.

"I thought I had you," the rider panted, and then he whipped up his snow goggles and squinted up at me with familiar dark brown eyes—the same dark brown I saw every morning in the mirror.

"Pax, every time I give you a head start you assume you'll beat me." I smiled down at my younger brother.

He sat up, unclipped one of his boots, and pulled his helmet off. Short black, sweaty hair stuck out in all directions. "Why do you have to stomp on a guy's hopes?"

I laughed. "If it makes you feel better, the only thing I was trying to stomp were those landings."

"You worry too much. You'll win the competition, and then fame and glory won't be far behind. Easy peasy." Pax unclipped his other boot and fell back on his elbows with a huge grin on his face. Braces lined his teeth, but they couldn't hide the chip on his front tooth from a skateboarding mishap. Not everyone in the Castillo clan is as athletically talented as my dad and I are.

"You make it sound so easy. Like recipe instructions." I appreciated his enthusiasm, but there was more to it than that. If I wanted to eventually go pro like our dad had, I had a lot more work to do.

"Yes! A recipe for success. You're welcome," Pax responded with a wink.

"Thanks." I shook my head again. "But I need to get in as many runs as possible over the next week before the competition." I looked back at the terrain park and the mountaintop. The gondolas on the ski lift glided up, growing smaller by the second. I wish I had time for one more run, but Mom would be expecting us home for dinner. I sighed. *There are never enough hours on the slopes.*

Pax stood. "Speaking of recipes, I'm hungry."

"When are you ever not hungry?" I responded, rolling my eyes.

Pax shrugged. "Good point."

"Come on, I want to stop by the ski shop

and pick up my new board." I unclipped my other boot and hoisted my board onto my shoulder. I'd shoveled more driveways and sidewalks than I could count to save up for this new board. Only the best equipment would get me a high score in the competition.

Pax followed me into the lodge. A blast of heat welcomed us, causing me to sweat almost immediately. Snow-drenched floor mats squished under our boots as we greeted a few riders on their way out for the day. The ski shop was empty besides two girls dressed in all white fur-trimmed parkas and matching white snow pants. Even their ski boots were a pristine white. Not a single scuff. *I just don't get it.* These two weren't snowboarders, more like snow bunnies—regulars who lived outside of town, mainly interested in looking good . . . and I wasn't referring to their skills or etiquette on the slopes.

As I walked up behind them they burst into a fit of giggles. I would've rolled my eyes at them if they could see me.

Ollie, the guy who practically lived at the

ski shop, didn't notice me either. It didn't help that the fur on the girls' parkas made them fluffier than the abominable snowman. I cleared my throat, announcing I was standing there. Of course, I might as well have been a pair of rental skis on a rack for all the attention I got from them. It wasn't until Pax scuffled in behind me that the party of three took notice.

"Jess, I'm starving. Grab your board and let's go," Pax whined.

Ollie's head popped up over the fur-trimmed hoods, and he nodded a hello. "Castillo, glad you stopped by." *Is that relief I see on his face?* We'd hung out in the shop and talked snowboarding enough times that I was pretty sure these girls weren't his favorite type of customer.

By the looks the two girls gave me, they didn't look too happy to see me. They turned back around and gave Ollie a few more giggles before they headed out the ski shop door.

"Bye, Oliver," one of the girls called over her shoulder before she disappeared into the hallway.

I raised an eyebrow at Ollie. His face flushed and he covered the back of his neck with his hand. "So, um, Oliver, is it? Do you think you could help an *actual* customer out?"

Ollie frowned. "Yeah, about that." He leaned on the back counter and set his gaze on me. For a millisecond I forgot why I'd walked in here. "You looked good out there today, Castillo."

"You were watching me?" I hoped my eyes weren't bugging out of my head.

Ollie shrugged. "I like to hit the slopes on my lunch break."

"Oh," I said, trying to sound casual.

"I mean, you are kind of hard to miss. No one shreds the slopes like that, and on the rails you have this style . . ." Ollie swiped his unruly hair away from his eyes. "It's . . . different."

I nodded, unsure if that was a compliment or not. If I was going to impress the judges at next week's competition, I'd have to land every trick. Maybe even harder tricks—different wasn't going to cut it. "Thanks," I said anyway.

"Yeah, you'll have to give me a tip or two."

"I guess so," I responded, hoping the blush I felt internally wasn't showing on my cheeks.

Ollie grinned wider. "Have you ever been on a backcountry trail?"

"No." I'd seen videos of riders on backcountry—untouched snow and natural terrain that stretched beyond the ski resort's mapped trails.

"You have to go. There's nothing like it if you're into more than groomed slopes."

"That sounds awesome." And it did. I'd tried nearly everything the snowboarding world had to offer. The slopes were my second home.

"How about on my next day off you show me some tips on those gnarly jumps you stomp, and I'll take you on a trail we don't show the tourists. It's a short hike off the expert run, but it's worth it. Plus it's easy to choose a route, not that I think *you'll* need help picking out a line. There are a couple of drops but enough ridges and patches of trees to break it up so you don't have to get down in one go."

My heart sped up.

"Are we even allowed over there?"

Ollie pushed off the counter and gave me a sheepish smile. "I wouldn't just take anyone," he said, leaning closer. My heart pounded a beat faster. I wasn't sure if it was Ollie's closeness or the fact I'd get to mark a backcountry run off my bucket list.

"I hate to interrupt this flirt sesh, but I'm hungry enough to take a bite out of my arm," Pax said, as he fell onto the front counter like he might faint from hunger.

I groaned inwardly. Leave it to Pax to turn an interesting conversation into a source of embarrassment for me.

"Right, you wouldn't happen to know if my board is in, would you?" I asked, changing the subject.

"About that. It won't be ready for you until tomorrow morning," Ollie said.

"Tomorrow?" I frowned. There was no hiding my disappointment. "It was supposed to be in last week."

"I know. I know. But some mega storm delayed our order. A new shipment comes in early tomorrow morning. It'll be in that," Ollie promised.

I forced a smile. "Yeah, of course. What's another day?" My dreams of becoming a professional snowboarder were worth the wait.

CHAPTER 2

The mouth-watering smell of garlic hit me
when I entered our front door. My stomach
grumbled in response. *Now* I was hungry. Pax
unlaced his boots and shoved them and his
jacket into the hall closet where we left our
gear to defrost. These had been Mama's rules
since we were little—no boards in the house or
boots beyond the entryway.

I hung up my snow pants before I followed
Pax into the kitchen. The table was already
set. My mom stood in front of the stove.
Nothing beat her cooking after a full day on
the slopes.

Pax reached for the refrigerator door at

the same time Mom said, "Don't even think about it. Dinner is almost done." Pax sighed and moped into the living room. I would never understand how Mom could catch us with her back turned.

"Where's Dad?" I eyed a salad on the counter next to my mom. I reached over, picked up a tomato, and popped it into my mouth.

"In the den." Mom swatted my hand away. "But not too much snowboard talk. Dinner will be ready in ten," she added as she pointed a wooden spoon at me.

I raised my hands in defense and gave Mom a sly smile. When it came to snowboarding, ten minutes was never enough.

Through the den doorway, the muffled sound of a sports channel greeted me. My dad stood in front of the large window, which overlooked a picturesque view of Crooked Peak Snow Resort.

From the doorway, I watched Dad trace the line of the mountain on the window. He didn't acknowledge me. Instead he started at the summit again and drew a new line like he could change the shape of the mountain with his fingertip.

"A storm is coming," he finally said without turning around.

The dusky sky was as clear as it had been that morning. Not a cloud in sight. Dad was always saying things about the snow conditions like he was a weather man—I was used to it. Not that I paid attention to whether he turned out to be right. Crooked Peak's snow-capped summits stood tall like jagged fingers ready to pierce the sky. I followed the line of the slopes with my eyes. I knew every inch of those courses by heart, maybe even with my eyes closed.

I joined him at the window and planted a kiss on his cheek. "What are you up to, Dad?"

"Fall lines." Dad traced the mountain again. He'd taught me about these routes, natural descents from the top of the mountain to the bottom, long before I rode my first one. He called them the paths of least resistance.

I stepped behind him and peered over his shoulder to get his perspective. His finger drifted over the cool glass beyond the resort's groomed slopes—down the center of the peak to the far left, around a large boulder, an edge that looked like a cliff. He drew a few more lines, harder routes with more difficult turns, before I broke the silence.

"You know Mom will go on a cleaning rampage when she sees all these fingerprints." I *tsk*ed just like my mom did when we made a mess.

"I know." Dad chuckled. "You see that part of the mountain? Where it juts out?" he asked and tapped the glass with this finger.

I nodded. It was barely visible in the fading light, but I knew the one. My dad had told me this story so many times I knew it word for word. It was my favorite.

"That's where I proposed to your mother."

"I can't believe you got her out there in the first place." I smiled. Mom was content to enjoy life fireside with hot cocoa in hand. The slopes she left up to the rest of the Castillo family.

Dad chuckled. "The only thing that worked was promising her a trip that didn't involve snow." Every vacation picture I had seen of my parents' life together revolved around my dad's competition schedule. Ski resort after ski resort.

I laughed alongside Dad. My mother was a stubborn woman—supposedly a quality every woman in our family inherited.

CHAPTER 3

Pax reached for a second helping of *pancit*, a steaming bowl of noodles with stir-fried chicken and veggies. Mom smiled. She prided herself on overfeeding anyone who walked into the Castillo household, and she wouldn't be denied. Many had entered our home, none had left hungry.

"I could eat my weight in this," Pax said, a few thin rice noodles hanging out of his mouth. Where he put all that food was a mystery to me. His fourteen-year-old frame remained lean and tall.

"Don't talk with your mouth full." By the tone of Mom's voice, anyone else would think she was scolding Pax. I knew better. She took Pax stuffing his face with her cooking as a compliment.

I wrinkled my nose at Pax before turning to Dad. "I had trouble landing a few five-forty spins today."

"It looked like you landed everything I saw," Pax said. He popped a peapod into his mouth.

"Well, that's because you can't count rotations. It ended up being three-sixty," I said. Sometimes I wished my brother would stay out of my conversations with Dad. He didn't take snowboarding seriously like we did.

"You know, Jessa, you're only sixteen. You have plenty of time to go pro—" Pax said between mouthfuls.

"Pax, your mother told you not to talk with your mouth full," Dad cut in.

"It takes hours of practice. Way more hours than I put in. I need to get in as much as I can before the competition." I looked to Dad to agree—he knew what it took to be the best of the best.

"School comes first, Jessa," Mom reminded me.

Of course it did. That was another one of Mom's rules since we were kids. Thank goodness it was winter break so there was no homework to get in the way right now.

"I have some thoughts on why I'm not getting enough rotation in the air," I said to Dad. "I'm going to get up early tomorrow and get in a few more runs before the weekend crowd hits the slopes. You know how it can get—"

Dad wiped his mouth with his napkin. "No."

I paused before I spoke. *Maybe I heard him wrong.* "No, you don't want to hear my thoughts? Or no, you don't know how packed the lifts get in the afternoon?"

"No, you're not going tomorrow."

"What? Why?"

"Jess, I admire your dedication. You have the Castillo spirit, I see it, but there's a storm coming in."

Again with this stupid storm. I stood up and crossed to the window. Whatever Mom and

Pax were saying came to a halt. "Dad, that is the clearest night sky I've seen in forever." I pointed at the front window, the night sky speckled with diamond-like stars. "This blizzard that you think is coming won't be here until tomorrow afternoon. By then I'll be back home," I said, hoping I wasn't coming off as disrespectful. I wasn't one to talk back to my parents, but this wasn't like Dad to not get it. I'd been waiting months to get on this new board, and no one was stopping me, especially not Mother Nature. "If this storm even comes at all," I muttered.

"Watch your tone," Dad said, his voice more calm and even than I expected. "I've lived around these mountains long enough to know the weather can change faster than you think."

"I don't get why you're making a big deal about the weather. I can handle the wind, and you know what it's like to ride on fresh snow." I gestured out the window to the slopes. "We live for the powder. It's not a superpipe, Dad. It's a silly storm—"

"Enough!" Dad stood, his jaw set hard. His uneven stance reminded me of the fall he took that put him through several surgeries followed by months of physical therapy. It took one superpipe injury to end his career. "You aren't going, and that's the end of it," he said with finality.

Suddenly winning this competition seemed even further out of my reach than I'd thought.

CHAPTER 4

I couldn't sleep. Every time I looked at the clock the blue digital numbers blinked back at me five minutes later. I groaned and stuffed my head under the pillow. *4:38 a.m. 4:43 a.m.* At this point I might as well get up. *And do what? Ride? Yeah, right.*

I pushed the curtains back from the window over my bed. Dawn was still an hour away, but the sky was as clear as it had been when Dad put me in my place last night. Guilt gnawed at my insides. Dad didn't deserve my outburst. Even after his accident he'd been supportive of my snowboarding journey.

I gazed at the mountain. Something stirred

in my stomach. I drew in a deep breath. I needed to have the snow beneath my board. I craved the weightlessness of flying through the air. I couldn't block out the small voice at the back of my mind: *Ride, Jessa.*

And just like that I was out of bed. What Dad didn't know wouldn't hurt him.

In the dark I pulled out the thermals and plush socks I wore under my jacket and pants—my favorite green and pink ones. I pulled my long black hair into a sloppy braid. *Am I actually going to do this? Sneak out?* I had never done it before, but I couldn't stop myself from walking down the hallway past my parents' bedroom.

The house was quiet. Thank goodness the soft lull of the heater covered the creak of the kitchen floor where I stepped. The plan was simple. I'd get to the resort, be ready the second the lifts opened, do one run on my favorite expert slope, hit the terrain park on the way down, and be back before a single cloud rolled in. *Easy peasy, as Pax would say,* I thought.

"Jessa?"

My heart skipped a beat. *Busted.* I blinked into the darkness of the kitchen until the soft blue of a cell phone screen glowed. "Pax, you scared me," I half-whispered, half-hissed.

"What are you doing up?"

"I should ask you the same question."

"I was hungry." Pax lifted a bowl of cereal into the light of his phone. The crunch of him chewing filled the silence before he spoke again. "Why are you dressed for . . ." His eyes widened. "No way, the golden child is going to break the rules."

"Whatever." I continued toward the entryway. I didn't need this right now.

"Dad is going to ground you for life," Pax whispered after me. "Mom will definitely break your board in two. She's small, but I bet she could do it."

I opened the hall closet and tugged on my pants and jacket by the glow of a nightlight. "Maybe. Or someone could be a good brother and cover for his golden-child sister."

"Really?" Pax watched me as I pulled on a fuzzy ski cap. "What am I going to say?"

"I don't know, make something up."

"Like what?" Pax shoved another spoonful of cereal into his mouth.

"Who knew I had two kids who were early risers?" a voice said in the dark. The hall light flipped on. Dad stepped into the entryway. And he didn't look pleased.

CHAPTER 5

Grounded for life. Pax's words echoed in my head. I could practically hear the snap of my board over my mom's knee. I wouldn't be able to talk myself out of this. I had my helmet in my hand. I thought frantically, trying to come up with any excuse that made sense. *Who takes their helmet to the grocery store? Oh yeah, I know. Me. You never know when you might slip in the parking lot—got to protect the noggin.*

"We're out of milk." Dad held up an empty plastic jug. "And cereal," he added, holding up an empty green box.

Maybe he hasn't noticed the helmet and snowboarding gear, I thought hopefully.

"Good going," I said to Pax, trying to act normal.

"What? I was hungry." Pax shrugged.

"Jessa." Dad's stern voice silenced us. Only the hum of the heater filled the air. By the crease of Dad's brow and the tight line of his lips, maybe grounded for life wouldn't be so awful. "I'm disappointed," he finally said. *So much for not noticing.*

"I'm sorry." An apology wasn't enough, but what else could I say?

Dad dropped his arms and the stern look on his face faded. "It's not like you to go behind my back, but it's more concerning that you'd put yourself in danger." His voice trailed off. He walked toward me, the hint of a limp visible. Back when the accident happened, I wasn't old enough to know what my parents went through, but I'd seen some of the recovery photos. "I expected more. I appreciate and admire your drive, it reminds me of me. Maybe it reminds me of me too much. You have my risky tendencies for putting the sport before your safety."

"Dad, I—"

He waved off my attempt at an explanation. "This is part of being a professional: knowing when to take risks, whether it's practice or competition, and knowing that your family comes first. That means staying safe. Your mother thought she'd lost me on that superpipe. I don't want to see her go through that again. Or worse."

"I wouldn't want all of you to go through that either. Dad, I . . ." I swallowed hard. *How can I make him see?*

"I understand you're trying to protect me. I'm grateful, for everything—teaching me to ride, showing me the ins and outs of the sport—it's just . . ." I took a deep breath. "I'm not you, Dad. I'm me. Jessamine," I whispered.

Dad blinked. I couldn't determine if I'd shocked him or gotten through to him. "Jessa, I see how important this sport is to you. Nothing stops a Castillo. It makes me think about how my own father would react if I'd tried to pull the same stunt you just did."

"Yeah?" *I think he gets it.*

Dad nodded. "I'd be off to my room with my head down and my tail tucked between my legs."

The energy drained from my body—*he didn't get it*. Here came the punishment. *Goodbye snowboarding career.*

"But I'm not him. And you're right, you're not me. So I'm allowing you to go this morning."

Did I hear him correctly? My dedication trumps my irresponsibility?

Pax gaped next to me.

Dad's face grew stern again. "I have two conditions." Of course he did. I released a slow breath. "There's been a shift in weather and it looks like the storm will hit later. I'm allowing you one run, and only one. My first condition is if you ever do this again when I've told you no you will not participate in the next competition. I don't care if it's the freaking X Games."

I nodded.

"You're also grounded starting after next week's competition. No going out, no skate park, and I'm confiscating your new board right after you compete."

"What?"

Dad raised an eyebrow, and I snapped my mouth shut.

"And my second condition—"

"But you already gave me two," I protested.

"I can make it three."

I pouted and crossed my arms in front of my chest. I had to stop myself from pointing out that his first condition had two parts. Next to me, Pax suppressed a smile. He had to be enjoying this—I was never in trouble.

"And you have to take Pax with you."

"What?" This time it was Pax's turn to complain. "I didn't do anything except finish off the milk."

"I can't take Pax with me," I said. "He'll slow me down."

"Gee, thanks," Pax said.

"I need to make sure you're safe up there. It'll keep you in line. Besides, if I don't get him out of here, he'll eat what's left of the food in the house."

"You know I'm standing right here," Pax said.

"Yep," Dad said turning to my brother. "And make sure you pick up a gallon of milk on the way home."

CHAPTER 6

"I think I forgot my phone," Pax said as he dug through his pockets.

"We're almost to the lodge. If I turn back now there's no way Dad will let us leave again." I guided my old pickup truck around a bend, both sides of the road lined with snow-covered pines. "Anyway, it's one run. Who do you need to call?"

Pax shrugged. "Fine. Let's just get up there so we can get back home."

Crooked Peak's Main Lodge rose in front of us, the steep angles of its roof came into view first. I pulled into the closest free parking space, one spot over from preferred parking.

Why was the lot practically empty? Sure we were early, but on most Saturday mornings, skiers and snowboarders were waiting outside before the lodge doors opened. *Oh well. Better for us—less wait time for lifts.* I climbed out of the truck and glanced back at my brother still seated in the cab.

"We're seriously going to do this?" Pax grumbled through his open window.

I ignored him and continued toward the lodge, a bounce in my step. The anticipation of riding the slopes never disappeared. Every time I walked into the lodge it was like the first time I stepped on a board as a little girl.

As we neared the entrance I gazed up at the mountains towering behind the lodge's roof. The slopes weren't yet dotted with skiers and snowboarders. I loved being here at this hour. I couldn't say the same for my brother.

I headed straight for the ski shop. I couldn't wait to get my hands on that new board, even if I only had it until the competition. I saw it before I even walked through the doorway. It took every ounce of willpower not to squeal. Ollie stood behind the counter with the gorgeous board propped next to him. He had on a bright blue Crooked Peak jacket. His unruly hair curled around the edges of his cap and collar. "As promised," he said.

"I was afraid you were going to leave me hanging again," I said with a huge grin on my face.

"Nope." Ollie placed the board on the counter. "I set up your bindings for you. You might have to adjust them some, but they should be close."

Not knowing what else to do I said thanks. Ollie stood across from me with only the counter keeping us apart. Both of our hands rested on the board. Too bad he was scheduled to work; having his company would've made my only ride of the day more fun. Instead I was stuck with grumpy Pax.

"Yeah, so this is romantic and all," Pax coughed, "but can we do this? My bed is calling to me, and if I have to follow you down that expert run we're going to be here all day. You know, with my slow skills and all. Besides, the beast will need to be fed again," he added with a pat to his stomach.

"You're going up to the top?" Ollie's brow crinkled.

"Yeah, I need to break in this board before next week." I lifted the board off the counter.

"I don't know if the gondolas are even running. You could probably get on an intermediate trail and the terrain park is open, but with the storm—"

"Ugh, you too? You sound like my dad."

Ollie chuckled. "I should probably take that as a dig, but being compared to *the* Ethan Castillo is a huge compliment. Anyway, if I could take you up there myself, I would."

"Man, you are my savior," Pax said to Ollie before turning to me and adding, "Let's go. I bet we could be home in time for mom's corned beef and side of fried eggs. I can smell the sizzle now."

"We're not leaving yet," I said, my eyes on Ollie.

"Wait, what?" Pax asked.

"Yeah." I smiled. "I think Ollie here just offered to give us guided admission to the top."

CHAPTER 7

Ollie's knee bounced up and down as the gondola drifted toward the summit. I'd never seen him nervous or fidgety like this before. He stared out the window. "I can't believe I'm doing this," he said.

"Neither can I," Pax grumbled. He kicked up his boots onto the empty seat next to me and slouched into his own. "He didn't have to work this hard to impress those girls talking to him at the shop yesterday," Pax said, looking straight at me.

"Pax!" Heat rushed to my cheeks. I wasn't trying to get Ollie to impress me, but it was too late. Pax's comment left us both shifting uncomfortably.

Ollie's hand went to the back of his neck, covering his own blush. "I wouldn't take you up if I didn't think you could handle the run."

Hoping to stifle the awkwardness in the air, I looked out the window at my view of the mountain. This side was ungroomed—dotted with sparse patches of trees, jutting boulders, and deep pockets in the slope that could be drops. From up here everything appeared small and peaceful. The gondola dipped before it slowed at the midpoint station making my empty stomach queasy. The operator nodded at Ollie in acknowledgement as our ride drifted past the stop.

"I'm sure she can handle the run," Pax muttered. "It's me I'm worried about."

* * *

The gondola swayed as we continued up. *Maybe I shouldn't have pushed Ollie to help me out. What if he gets in trouble? Or worse, fired?* The gondola operator at the top was hesitant to let us off. But somehow, Ollie convinced him that we wanted to check out the ride lines and the view since the slopes were closing down early today. We'd come right back afterward. A little small talk and a few fist bumps later, we were on our way.

"I have to head back down," Ollie said once we were out of sight of the gondola operator. He glanced toward the large viewing window of the Summit Lodge at the top of the mountain. It was the last station where you could grab a bite or use the facilities before riding down the resort's largest peak. A pale blue sky overcast with a thin layer of clouds waited for us outside. "The storm is delayed, but you should try to get down the slopes quickly. Stop by the shop when you're done."

"Yeah, thanks. I owe you one." I smiled.

"I know." Ollie grinned back before he headed to the gondolas and caught a ride down to the main lodge. I didn't look at Pax, but I was sure he'd given the biggest eye roll possible. For once I wished it was cold enough for his face to freeze that way.

I waved goodbye and stepped through the doors of the Summit's viewing platform. The whistle of icy air rushed past my ears. I tugged my ski cap down. Although clouds covered every inch of sky, the surrounding peaks took my breath away. Black and gray rock frosted in white. No matter how many times I stood on the summit, it never failed to make every part of my body buzz with excitement.

I inhaled deeply and let the mountain air ice my lungs. *Freedom.*

The click of Pax's bindings snapped me back into reality. He pulled on his ski gloves and I did the same. I slipped my boots into the bindings of my new snowboard and tightened them. *Near perfect. How did Ollie know?* A small smile crept onto my lips. I rocked back and forth until my stance settled in and made a few minor adjustments. *Too bad he isn't here to join me.*

Pax and I made our way over to where the run started, the snow crisscrossed with ski and snowboard lines. Pax reached for his goggles. "Let's do this," he said. I nodded.

"Hey, what are you kids doing up here?" a voiced called out. We turned back to the gondola station where a Crooked Peak security guard walked toward us. "This trail is closed."

CHAPTER 8

Just go.

The same voice that convinced me to sneak out this morning coaxed me to grab Pax by the sleeve and yank him down the slope. What would the guard do? Go after us? He wasn't on skis. My gaze darted from the security guard to the peak's edge to Pax and back to the security guard.

"Don't even think about it," Pax said under his breath. He shook his head, and I hesitated. The window of opportunity for escape passed.

The guard headed over to us. "I don't know how you got up here, but this trail is closed. There's supposed to be a storm coming in fast."

I would've mentioned he also sounded like my dad, but I had a feeling he wouldn't be as impressed as Ollie by being compared to Ethan Castillo. I also could've told him I knew this trail better than most of the instructors, but I was sure that wouldn't change his mind either. "I'm going to radio the gondola operator to take you back down."

"Yeah, sure, thanks." I grabbed Pax's ski jacket sleeve and gave the guard my best angelic smile. "Let's go wait on the platform, little brother."

Pax narrowed his eyes at me. He knew I was up to something. "Just a second ago you looked willing to push me down the mountain to get in a run—"

I shushed him. "Don't look back. Act like one of those lost tourists."

"Lost what? I don't know what you're up to, but I have a feeling it's going to get us into a lot of trouble." Pax followed me along the board and boot prints leading back to the Summit

Lodge. When I reached the door I turned and waved at the security guard. Satisfied, the guard waved back and continued his patrol of the mountaintop. As soon as his back was turned, I yanked Pax around the entrance to the platform. "This way, hurry."

"Where are we going?" he asked. I glanced over my shoulder. *If the guard had seen us, we would've heard him by now.* "Jessa, I'm talking to you," Pax hissed at me.

"Trust me."

By now we were on the other side of the station where the mountaintop stretched in a gradual downward slope. It wasn't steep enough to gain any momentum, but it was right where I wanted to be. Signs marked with arrows directed us back in the direction we'd come.

"Trust you? If you haven't noticed, this isn't a trail. Did you not see the 'Do Not Enter' sign?" Pax stopped and looked around him. "There's not even boot or board tracks here."

"I saw it, and yes, I know." I turned around and walked away from him. Snow crunched beneath my boots, untouched by human tracks. "But I know where we're going. I promise you it'll be fun—it'll be worth it."

Pax huffed, a white billow of his breath forming around his face. He glanced up. Cloud cover blocked the sun and every last inch of blue sky, and the temperature had definitely dropped. Still, the weather didn't seem that threatening to me.

He picked up his board and followed behind me. "What could possibly be fun about a trail no one's ever gone down before?"

I smiled and continued my trek forward. This wasn't the same smile I gave the security guard, and it definitely wasn't the same smile Ollie put on my face. This one was fueled by pure adrenaline. "That's exactly what makes it more fun. To stand above the world, untouched, and find the perfect line. New scenery, natural obstacles and terrain. Just us and the mountain."

Pax wrinkled his brow. "That doesn't sound very fun to me."

I stopped and looked toward the sprawling

mountainside farther across the peak. Pax followed my gaze. Smooth, flawless snow covered every inch of rock except for the sprinkling of protruding boulders and winding patches of spruce trees that disappeared halfway down the mountain into a white abyss. "That's where we're going. Backcountry."

CHAPTER 9

"Backcountry? This is dangerous," Pax said, drawing my attention away from the awesome view. "What has gotten into you?"

"Nothing, and it's not dangerous. Besides, you heard Ollie, he says he trusts me. I can handle this." Maybe Pax would struggle, but that's why I was here—to help my baby brother.

Pax shook his head. "He didn't say he trusts you to go down an untouched trail. I'm going back."

"What? No, you can't," I blurted out.

"Jess, I'm pretty sure I can. I just turn around and—"

"No, you can't because . . ." I dug for a

reason that didn't include a sudden twinge of fear about being out in the middle of nowhere alone. That was silly. When it came to snowboarding it was only me, my board, and the snow. But now, looking at all of the uncarved powder had my stomach in knots. *What is wrong with me?* I hadn't felt that way since I made my first jump. I shook off the doubt. "Because Dad told you that you had to."

Pax jutted out his chin in a pout. I had him.

He trudged past me, making new boot prints in the trail ahead. "You know, I have to admit I liked it better when you were the golden child. This new rebel personality of yours is more work for me than I expected. It's almost as if we've switched titles; now I'm the golden child and you're the troublemaker."

I smiled and followed my brother. "Don't get used to it. I'm only lending you the title."

Pax laughed. Although he was only a few feet in front of me, the wind picked up and carried his laughter down the mountain. I shivered and zipped my jacket to the top so it shielded my mouth from the icy wind.

I glanced back at the sky behind us. The white cloud cover remained above our heads blocking out the sun, but grayer skies hovered over neighboring peaks.

The storm wouldn't catch us—if that was the storm. *We have plenty of time. Right?*

I set my sights on the path ahead. Ten more minutes and we'd reach the end of the trail, where a group of trees hugged a flatter portion of the adjoining mountain peak like a shallow platform. From there I could figure out the best line, ride down the mountain, and be back at the lodge before lunch.

"You know, it's actually pretty cool we're doing this," Pax said after we'd walked along the trail in silence for a few minutes.

"Oh yeah?" I couldn't hide my surprise. "I thought it was too dangerous," I teased.

Pax shrugged. "Yeah, it probably is. And there's a chance I'll get eaten by a mountain lion."

"I doubt it," I said.

"I watch a lot of nature TV." Pax readjusted his board on his shoulder. "We're in nature's territory now. This is prime hunting grounds.

If I was a mountain lion that lived out here with nothing but snow, I'd be hungry."

I threw a nervous glance toward the patch of trees ahead of us. Ollie had never mentioned anything about wild animals. "Can we cool it on the prey-of-wild-animals talk?"

"Yeah, sure." Pax stopped and set his board down once we hit the patch of trees. "I'm just saying if it weren't for you I'd never have a chance at something like this. So thanks. Maybe being the little brother of the golden child isn't so bad after all."

"So I've regained my title already then?" I raised an eyebrow.

"Well, there is only room for one rebel in this family and that's me." Pax grinned at me, then walked through the small grove of trees to where the ground gave way to the slope of the mountain. Wind swirled snow across the descending rock. When Dad had traced the mountain lines from the window yesterday, I'd remembered every line clearly in my head, but from up here the path wasn't as easy. The snowfall messed with my depth perception and I couldn't gauge how far the drops would be off each cliff. "Having second thoughts?" Pax asked.

It'd be a challenge, but the voice of doubt in the back of my head remained silent. "Nope." I took out my phone and snapped a few shots of the view. My phone battery showed 99 percent.

"Then as the official Castillo troublemaker, I say it's time to ride," he said. "No turning back now."

CHAPTER 10

I stood on the edge of one of the biggest rides
of my life. *Ollie was right*, I reassured myself.
Even though I didn't have any experience
backcountry riding, he trusted my skill and
so did I. Before me lay two thousand feet of
untouched snow, and it would be me, Jessamine
Castillo, carving it up. "They don't call me
Shredder for nothing," I whispered to myself.

Another gust of wind whipped around us
and dusted snow across our path. I brushed off
my jacket, and the wind picked up more. Beside
me, Pax shivered.

"Are you okay?" I asked.

"If I would've known it'd be snowing

during this ride I would've worn more layers," Pax said.

"Snowing?" I looked behind me—the ashen sky had caught up to us. The wind wasn't picking up fallen snow off the side of the mountain like I had thought. It was full-on coming down out of the sky. The storm was closing in. "We need to get down."

"You think?" Pax asked dryly.

I shot him a now-is-not-the-time look and focused back on the mountainside. I had to pick a line quickly and relay it to my brother so we could outride this storm.

"C'mon, Jess, tell me the plan before I turn into a snowman." Pax tightened his bindings and wrestled with his gloves. In my family, Pax was known for his lax attitude about, well, everything, but for once, all calm had left him.

"I'm thinking," I said. I took in the steepness of the slope. If we rode the fall line, making turns on either side of it, we'd hit the first patch of trees with controllable speed. Maybe. No doubt there'd be drops along the next section, but the large rocks dotting the middle of the slope made good reference points. If only I could see what came after the second patch of trees . . .

I didn't know this terrain like I knew my favorite expert trail or every feature in the terrain park. And I wasn't positive Pax could make these jumps. I wished I had asked Ollie more questions about backcountry riding.

"Well, think faster." Pax rocked back and forth on his board. His energy crept into my body and sped up the thud of my heart. The pulse of my blood in my ears drowned out the howl of the wind. I couldn't focus.

"Can you stop that?" I snapped. Pax stopped rocking on his board, crossed his arms in front of his chest, and sank into a slouch like an unhappy child. *Think, Jessa, think.* The snow fell heavier, speckling my braid, but I could navigate this—I had to trust my instincts. If anything, fresh powder was the best way to ride. "I got it."

Pax stood at attention, relief softening his brow. "Lay it on me."

"There." I pointed to the next smattering of trees below us. This was the line. "The mountain levels off enough for us to slow down. Stay more to the left until you get to the trees, it's less steep. Below that it looks like there are a couple of drops, but you should be able to land those if you stay the course and keep your speed down." I glanced at him, hoping he was down for this plan. "It looks like a smooth ride, but I don't know how rocky it is beneath this snow."

"Easy peasy." Pax sounded like his usual chill self. Relief washed over me. Maybe my brother could pull this off.

"Great. Once we hit the second section of trees, the pine forest above the base of the mountain, we might have to hike through it on foot. With the lack of visibility from here, I won't know until we reach it, but the rest should be a laid-back ride."

"Got it." Pax said and slid down his goggles from the front of his helmet to cover his eyes. I stared at my reflection in his mirror-like lenses. A fearless girl with a wind-tussled braid hanging out the bottom of her helmet stared back. *That's me—I just have to remember that.*

Then my brother rocked forward on his board and propelled himself down the mountain. "Race you to the bottom!" he called over his shoulder.

CHAPTER 11

I stood at the summit alone, a stone the size of my fist nestled in the pit of my stomach. I was anything but fearless—panicked came to mind. *What was Pax thinking?* I kept my eyes on his descending figure as I slid my boots into my bindings and tightened them. *Don't lose him, don't lose him.* I yanked my goggles over my eyes and leaned over the edge of the slope. The nose of my board tipped down, the scrape of fresh powder against new fiberglass sent a chill over my skin. Snow rushed past me as I bent my knees and picked up speed.

Ahead of me, Pax came in and out of his turns faster and sloppier, but somehow he managed to stay upright on his board. I could catch him. I just had to get to him before he hit one of those drops. From the gondolas, those drops were non-threatening beginner jumps, ones I cleared no problem on my first terrain runs as a young girl. Here and now, the perception was different; they were cliff-like drops, where a second of air time felt like an eternity.

I leaned into my turn and cut into the newly fallen snow. I bent my knees more and lowered my stance, snow pelting my bare cheeks. Boy, did I love the burn of the wind. Since we'd never been on this trail, we should've taken it more slowly than our usual runs, but every other turn Pax seemed to be handling his board fine. He landed the small rises and falls of the downward slope, to my relief. Any other time I'd be proud of his improvement and adventurous nature.

I gained on my brother. I leaned into the front edge of my board then on the back edge and front again until I found my rhythm. As I maneuvered around a large uncovered boulder,

I swung wide and skimmed the surface of the snow with my fingertips to keep my balance. I took a small jump and grabbed the bottom of my board once I hit air. I stomped down, and I caught up with Pax.

"Pax!" My brother crossed in front of me unaware I was on his tail. I raised my stance and slowed so I wouldn't plow into him. The first patch of trees were coming up, and we needed to stop there so I could confirm we were on the safest route. "Pax!" I called again. "Hold up!"

This time Pax's head turned to the right. "No way. I got this."

"Pax, this is dangerous." I managed to stay at his pace.

"So now it's dangerous?"

"Slow down! You don't know what's up ahead."

"I know what I'm doing. So far so good," Pax called to me. But he had *no* idea—he was all over the place—at this pace he wouldn't be able to control his board when we came up on the trees. He turned his head in my direction again and gave me two thumbs up. Then he wobbled on his board, regained his balance, and wobbled again.

"Yeah, sure looks like it."

"Whatever." Pax crouched lower and moved a snowboard's length ahead of me.

I followed. "What's gotten into you?"

"Just beating my sister." Pax threw me a devious smile and leaned in to his turn until the edge of his board carved deep into the snow.

When did he learn that? I straightened slightly, both shocked and impressed.

No way would he show me up. I bent my knees and caught up to Pax again. The steepness of the slope tapered off and a sprinkling of pine trees rose around us. Pax turned in and out of the patches of spruce. He wasn't slowing.

"Pax!" I called. The small grove of trees thinned. Ahead a smooth downward slope appeared, the edge of it disappearing into nothingness—the first drop. It would be the shortest of the ones ahead of us, but Pax didn't seem like he knew he was riding straight for it.

Pax took the slope without a single hesitation. *He couldn't possibly know*, I worried.

"Pax, stop!" The icy winds swept my words over the cliff along with my brother. I was too late.

CHAPTER 12

One second Pax was there and the next
he wasn't.

"No!" I screamed as I crouched lower,
readying myself to take the jump and follow my
brother into the white oblivion below. I couldn't
save him, so all I could do was follow him. This
was my fault. The edge of the drop met the toe
of my board and I was airborne. The ground
appeared beneath me, endless white. My stomach
knotted until the weightlessness of the freefall
grabbed me.

I viewed Pax in front of me as he fell in slow
motion, arms flailing. Snow sprayed in the air
when Pax's board finally hit the base of the

drop. For a second the snow blinded me and then Pax reappeared. He sailed forward still upright before he tumbled head-over-board twice and landed in a lump several yards in front of me.

"Pax!" I yelled, as I landed the jump hard. I skidded to a halt next to him and ripped off the buckles of my bindings. Pax wasn't moving. I dropped to my knees next to him, his arms splayed to his sides. Nothing appeared to be broken, but who could tell with all the snow gear. "Talk to me," I cried and yanked up my brother's goggles off his eyes.

Pax blinked, eyes wide, and stared past me. He didn't say anything.

"Pax?" I waited, a lump formed in my throat. The worst outcomes filled my thoughts. A brain or spinal injury. I wanted to grab his jacket and shake him into speaking.

"I'm alive." Pax uttered and then drew in a deep breath. He threw arms above his head and pumped his fists into the air. "I'm alive!"

"You jerk! I thought I'd lost you." I didn't know whether to be relieved or upset.

Pax sat up. "Did you see that? I landed the jump. Sort of. It was gnarly, but I made it."

"Yeah, I saw it. I fell right behind you, remember?"

"Oh man, it was incredible." Pax howled into the sky above. Snow fell heavy on his face, white dotting his dark eyelashes. "I flew right off that cliff like a bird!" He flapped his arms.

I wished I could rejoice with him, but my visibility was decreasing with the snowfall. I looked around at the mountainside. We were only a quarter of the way down, and at this rate we wouldn't be able to see the base of the mountain soon. "We need to keep going."

Pax pulled himself up. "I'm ready. You don't have to tell me twice." He added a few more fist pumps.

With a better view of what was ahead of us than I'd had up top, I picked a new course for us to take down. Again I identified the natural landmarks and the lines Dad had traced last night in the den. I just needed to pick the safest route I could see. Once I was sure, I relayed the plan to Pax and made him promise he'd take it easy on this next run.

We both unclipped our rear boot from our bindings and scooted along the flat section of snow until the slope descended again. Pax stopped next to me, and we both retightened our bindings and adjusted our goggles. I looked back at our tracks on the upper part of the mountain, but the snow had started to fall more heavily, blanketing them. Swiveling my head, I looked down the mountain toward the bottom. From this point, the thick forest of pines at the base of the mountain was still visible through the snow. *But for how long? And will we be able to see the drops before we hit them?* I wondered.

Pax nodded he was ready. We both rocked forward and tipped the head of our boards downslope. This time Pax stayed at the pace I set. With the dull gray sky blocking out the sun, I had to put all my concentration on the landscape below. It would be harder to spot jutting rocks or changes in the terrain.

I glanced at Pax, and he gave me a show of

an exaggerated yawn. I had to agree with him. This was nowhere near the speed I traveled on my usual runs. That familiar voice telling me to push the limits whispered to me. I nodded toward our destination, and Pax flipped me two thumbs-up. I bent my knees to pick up velocity and he followed, matching my speed. Our boards carved out crisscrossing lines across the blank slate of snow.

Wind rushed past my head in a flurry of snowflakes. With this section of the mountain clear of visible obstacles, I couldn't resist pushing the speed on my new board. *I could slow down and signal to Pax before the next drop*, I thought as I picked up speed. I leaned my weight from one edge of my board to the other and back. Ahead a slight rise in the slope created the perfect ramp for a jump—there was no holding back. I sailed off it in a three-sixty and landed it like a pro. Adrenaline filled every inch of my veins. *The next incline I'll add a hand grab, maybe even push for a five-forty if I can get enough height on my jump*, I thought excitedly.

"Pax, did you see that . . ." I started to say as I checked over my shoulder. But my words died on my lips before the wind could carry them away. I came all the way up on my board's edge and halted. Pax was gone.

CHAPTER 13

I stared up at the mountain and waited. My ragged breathing left puffs of white clouds around my head. "Pax!" I called. Nothing. "Pax!" I squinted through the snow, which was now coming down in a thick curtain of white. *C'mon, c'mon, Pax, show up.* He had to be right behind me. I'd been going faster than I thought—he just couldn't keep up.

Any second now.

Still nothing.

I loosened my bindings and stepped into the snow. My weight sank me boot-deep until I hit the packed snow beneath. "Pax, if you hear me, say something," I called out. What if he was injured or had gotten lost? Dread crept into my veins. *Stop it, Jessa.* I couldn't think that way. *Maybe he passed me.* No, that wasn't possible either—I would've seen him.

I couldn't stand there and wait for him all day—the snow would bury me. I had to find him, and the only way was up. The climb wasn't ideal lugging my board, but it could've been worse. As I made my way up the slope I called out for my brother and kept an eye out for a second set of board tracks. My tracks were still visible as I continued up the slope—I wasn't sure if a non-existent second set was a good or a bad thing. Pax could be reckless, but he wouldn't stray from following me too much. The path I had taken was free of large rocks and trees. He's smart enough not to choose his own way down.

Bursts of wind rushed past me, and I had to stop to maintain my balance. The storm was on me and I didn't know how bad it was going to get. If this was its worst, I still had a good chance of finding Pax. The weight of my fears lifted with that one thought. But my board was another story. It was lighter than my old one, but climbing against the wind I might as well have been carrying a cinder block.

"Pax!" I cried again, my voice rough. The icy winds scraped at my throat every time I called for my brother. The wind howled back—and still no Pax. I set my board down. I didn't know how long I'd been searching, but up here surrounded by white in every direction, it felt like time stood still. I pulled off a glove, unzipped the pocket of my jacket where I kept my phone, and dug it out. My thumb hovered over the home button as the winds chilled my bare skin. My eyes stung. *How will Mom take the news?*

Crunch. Crunch.

I whipped around toward the sound and searched the slope. "Pax? Are you out there?" For a moment the wind stopped; my breath was loud in my ears.

Crunch.

I opened my mouth to call out his name again but stopped myself. My skin prickled and a new worry drifted into my thoughts.

What if Pax was right? Maybe someone walking through the snow wasn't a som*cone* but a some*thing*.

I didn't dare move. When I'd stood at that summit with the storm at my back, a wild animal attack had sounded impossible. Now I couldn't shake the idea from my head. I wasn't prepared for that. What if that was the reason Pax hadn't made it down?

Crunch. Crunch.

I froze, the thud of my heart heavy in my ear, and out of the heavy snowfall two rabbits hopped farther up the slope across my fading snowboard line. Relief loosened my stance. Each jump swallowed the rabbits until they hopped into another snow drift. *Crunch. Crunch.* They disappeared again. I couldn't handle a mountain lion, but snow bunnies were fine by me.

And that's when I saw it. Several yards up the slope behind my new friends, I spotted a deep blue lump on top of the snow.

With newfound energy I hoisted my board up and took huge leaping steps uphill. My furry friends scattered, and I dashed across the slope to the right of my snowboard tracks. As I had hoped, it belonged to Pax—one of his ski gloves. "Pax," I called with renewed hope. My gaze darted back and forth over the mountainside, squinting through the swirling snow. There, a few yards even farther to the right were boot prints and board tracks like the board had been dragged.

"Pax!" I ran toward his tracks—well, my version of running—as I hurdled over the shallow drifts of snow lugging a snowboard caught by updrafts of wind.

The boot prints led to a sparse patch of pines, their trunks leaning downslope from the constant beating of the wind. Huddled between them in an alcove formed by jutting rock was Pax.

CHAPTER 14

I stopped once I was close enough to Pax to see him clearly. His eyes were closed and snowflakes clung to his lashes. He sat on a cushion of pine needles, his arms wrapped tight around his knees and a slight blue tinge to his lips. A tight knot formed in my stomach.

"Are you hurt? What happened?" I asked as I knelt at his side and touched the sleeve of his jacket.

Pax opened his eyes and shivered. "No, I didn't fall. I had to stop. I don't know what happened. You pulled ahead and I tried to stay behind you. One minute I was following your tracks and the next they were gone. It was just white everywhere. I couldn't tell if I was going up or down." Pax shivered again. He looked past me, a confused gleam to his eyes.

"Let's get you up. You shouldn't be sitting on the ground, it's too cold." I helped him up and he continued shivering. "How did you get over here?"

"I stopped and thought I'd call you, but I realized I didn't bring my phone," Pax said.

Guilt nipped at my insides. I'd told him he didn't need his phone, that we'd be home before lunch.

I wrestled my jacket sleeve up and checked my watch. 9:34 a.m. Mom wouldn't be expecting us home yet. I imagined her in the kitchen putting away the morning dishes. Dad in the recliner with his feet propped up and a sports channel on.

"It's fine. We're here together. Let's just get down this mountain."

Pax was still shaking. "Good idea."

"Are you okay?" I couldn't hide the concern on my face, but maybe Pax wouldn't hear it in my voice.

"Is it just me or is it really cold?" Pax said through chattering teeth.

Sure my cheeks were windburned, and it wasn't one of those days I could get away with snow pants and a thin jacket over my hoodie, but my thermals did their job. "What are you wearing under your jacket?"

Pax took a shaky hand and unzipped his coat half way. A navy crew neck stared back at me.

"Pax, why aren't you dressed to snowboard?"

"It's a long sleeve." Pax zipped his jacket back up. "This wasn't my idea in the first place. I just wanted a bowl of cereal. Speaking of—I could scarf down an entire box right about now."

I sighed and reached into the right pocket of my snow pants. When I snowboarded on the resort I preferred to carry as little as possible, but I'd have to admit to Mom that her idea of an emergency stash came in handy. I never used the pocket warmers so I crossed my fingers and hoped they weren't expired.

"Here, put these in the inside pockets of your jacket," I said, handing Pax one package while I opened the other.

"Awesome. Chest warmers." Pax wagged his eyebrows at me.

"Glad you still have your sense of humor intact." I slid my gloves back on. "Let's go."

"Jess . . ."

"Yeah?"

Concern lined his face. "I don't think it'll be that easy."

I looked over my shoulder to where my brother pointed. The storm had worsened. We were in a complete whiteout.

CHAPTER 15

I willed the forest at the base of the mountain
to appear, but for all the squinting in the world
I could've been looking at a white sheet of paper.

Luckily, the rocks above sheltered us from
the worst of the winds and the bent pines
next to us took the brunt of the snow. Pax
folded his arms across his chest and tucked his
hands under his armpits. The pocket warmers
appeared to help, but who knew how long
those would last. The cold crept into my boots,
and if I could see my nose I was sure there'd be
icicles hanging off of it. There was no telling
when this storm would end and if we'd outlast
it before we froze into ice pops.

"Tell me you have a plan," Pax said. My silence was enough. "You don't, do you?"

"No, but I have a phone." I pulled it out of my pocket and jabbed my thumb at the home button. "I'll call the Main Lodge and get Ollie to send someone out here to find us. We're not too far off the route. I know about where we're at."

I tapped the ski shop in my recent calls and waited. "Calling . . ." appeared on my screen—followed by a low battery notification. "How is that possible?" I closed the notification and put the phone up to my ear. No ring.

"What? Is no one answering?" Pax asked anxiously.

"It's not even connecting." The battery indicator blinked red with *12 percent* in the upper right corner of my screen. "It doesn't make any sense. I had a full charge after we left the gondolas."

Pax glanced up at the rock overhang above our heads. "There's probably no signal. At the top of the mountain you had all your bars, but here, the battery is drained from searching. We have to get out in the open."

"We'll freeze to death," I responded. *I can't believe he is actually suggesting that,* I thought.

"Not much difference if we stay here."

I stared out at the endless white surrounding us. *He's right.* We'd have to leave our shelter until we found a signal. What if we couldn't find our way back? Or my phone died?

"What's the worst that could happen? We'd fall off a cliff?" Pax added.

That was the next question I was about to ask myself.

CHAPTER 16

"Jess."

My brain filed through everything Dad had taught me about the mountains, picking the perfect line, and the subtle nuances of snowboarding—gems that he'd discovered through years of experience. *Maybe he said something important, and I wasn't listening. There has to be something.*

"Jess!" This time Pax got my attention.

"Pax, I've got nothing. There's a good chance we could go in the wrong direction and walk right off the side of this mountain. Or never find a signal, wander the mountainside for hours, and end up with hypothermia." I hadn't wanted to say any of those scenarios out loud, but it was true.

"Well, I think I already have the hypothermia thing down." Pax forced a smile.

"That's not funny."

A strong gust of wind swept into our alcove and whipped frozen snow at us, scraping my already raw cheeks. We stepped deeper under the protection of the rocky cliff above us and huddled closer together. The strengthening storm and the weight of the snow loosened a massive clump from the jutting rocks overhead and sent it tumbling where we had stood. Pax gaped at me, his eyes wide with shock. I had no doubt my expression mirrored his.

"That was close," Pax said and peered out hesitantly from beneath the alcove above our heads. "Like a mini avalanche."

Another natural disaster I hoped we didn't run into.

Outside of our alcove the pile of fallen snow rose up like a miniature mountain. We couldn't see anything other than the few yards in front of us.

"I don't think if you stare at the snow long enough you'll be able to burn a hole through it," Pax said. He gave me a crooked smile. "But that'd be a cool superpower. We'd at least be warm."

"Wait, you just gave me an idea." I walked closer to the edge of our protective space. My eyes remained on the snow.

"I was kidding about the superpower thing." Pax shivered. "Look who's losing it now. Maybe I should worry about how bad your hypothermia is."

I ignored my brother's attempt at keeping our situation light and grabbed a handful of snow. My fist closed around the fresh snow, and when I opened my hand up again the wind took the soft flakes away. "That won't work," I muttered. I brushed away the top layer of snow from the mini mountain until I got to the harder layer below. I dug in and packed a handful into a tight ball.

"A snowball fight? That's your plan?" Pax frowned. He threw up his arms in defeat. "The golden child has lost her mind."

"Pax, could you just trust me for once?"

"Yeah, I did, Jess," he said with a smirk. "I went with you on this crazy dangerous backcountry run without a guide and now you want to throw snowballs around."

He's got a point.

"I'm sorry, Pax." And I meant it. Dad was right—I had to choose my family first. I put my brother in danger and myself, but I would make it up to him.

Pax nodded. For all his jokes, he knew how serious the situation was. He was afraid. "It's cool. I guess if I'm going to freeze to death, I'd rather do it with you."

"Um, thanks?" I gave Pax a reassuring smile. "I'm glad I'm here with you, too, but I'm not going to let us freeze to death."

I aimed the snowball a few feet out of our shelter and threw it. It plopped into the snow ahead of us, but I could still see where it was. "Yes."

"I'm not sure what you are trying to do, but if this is a distance contest you didn't get too far."

"It's not. It's a point of reference," I said. Pax looked at me like I had two heads. "If you throw it too far it'll be lost in the blizzard, but if you toss it in front of you and see where it lands you know up to that point its safe. If the snowball went over the mountain—"

"—it's a cliff," Pax chimed in.

I grinned. *He got it.*

Pax dusted off a patch of snow next to him and scooped up the hard packing snow beneath. "Then let's get this snowball fight rolling."

CHAPTER 17

We made slow progress.

We couldn't carry our boards and roll snowballs at the same time. One foot strapped to the board was awkward too. The best we could come up with was keeping our boards leashed to our leg. The resort required anyone on their trails to wear a cord around their leg that clipped to their board to prevent the board from sliding downhill when they stepped in and out of their bindings. This was the only time I was thankful for that rule, but dragging a snowboard wasn't too much different than walking a dog that was walking his owner.

Our snowboards either got caught up in the terrain behind us or it slid in front of us when the slope steepened.

Pax stayed an arm's length to my right. No way would I lose him this time. I kept my phone off to preserve what little battery life I had left. I hoped when I turned it back on we'd have a location with enough bars to contact the Main Lodge.

"How are you doing?" I asked when I noticed Pax's pace slow.

He tossed another snowball out in front of us. "Tired. And my toes feel numb. Actually my whole face feels numb."

I licked my wind-chapped lips, the dry skin rough beneath my tongue. The wind blew furiously around us. Sometimes it pelted us with snowflakes-turned-frozen-ice and other times the wind felt like icy fingers that gripped me through my layers of clothes—layers my brother didn't have.

"Let's stop and check my signal." We turned to each other until our helmets touched and shielded the phone with our bodies. I restarted my phone and waited for the screen to power up—12 percent battery life. Two bars appeared in the left corner. *Yes.* I tapped the ski shop and "Calling" appeared on the screen again. "Please work. Please work." Silence filled the phone pressed to my ear.

"Anything?" Pax asked.

"Not yet." I checked the bars—still there. Finally, the best sound in the world filled my ear. The phone rang. "It's ringing." And rang. And rang. And rang.

"Well?"

"No one's picking up," I said as dread filled my mind.

"They can't be closed. Ollie knows we didn't stop by the shop yet." Pax pulled away, his breath heavy. "They can't close the lodge with us still up here. Right? Can they?"

"Calm down." I reached for my brother's arm and he pulled out of my reach. The phone clicked in my ear like someone picked up. "Wait. Hello?" As if the wind knew I was close to escape, it picked up, forcing to me to turn and brace against it.

"What are they saying?" Pax called, shielding himself as well.

"Hello?" Between my brother and the howl of the wind I couldn't tell if it was a bad connection or I couldn't hear the other person on the line. "Hello?"

"Jess—"

"—don't freak out on me now, Pax." The phone beeped in my ear with another message box: 5 percent battery. Power save mode.

"I don't know what else to do. We can't survive out here." Pax's shoulders sagged in defeat. "All I know is I'm cold and tired. I can't feel my feet or my hands, and I'm so hungry at this point I'd eat that liver dish mom makes."

Even with Pax's goggles covering half his face, it couldn't hide his hopelessness. I had put him here, and I didn't know if I could get him out. I wished I had something to say, some way to fix this, but the truth was I didn't.

Pax must've seen it in me. Without another word he turned and walked down slope, past the last snowball he threw, with his snowboard trailing him.

"Where are you going? You can't just walk ahead. You can't even see where you're going!" I shielded my face against the wind with my arm.

"Does it even matter anymore, Jess?" Pax trudged forward.

"It does. Maybe someone is looking for us. Maybe Ollie assumed we were lost when we didn't show up." I followed after him. The strain of wading through the rising snow and endless wind drained me with each step. I wasn't even sure I believed my own words. Would a rescue team even risk more lives to find us in a whiteout?

Pax stumbled in front of me. When I helped him up, he swatted me away and continued his trek into nothingness. With his every step I half expected him to disappear before my eyes. Somehow we slogged forward in the storm. Every yard of progress brought another inch of numbness into my limbs. I focused on Pax's snowboard as it slid through and skittered over the snow.

White, white, and more white. I couldn't even tell if we were going anywhere anymore.

It was like we were walking on one of those moving walkways in the airport terminals except in the wrong direction. If we stopped maybe it would carry us back to the top of the mountain. I entertained myself with the thought until a dark silhouette appeared out of the corner of my eye.

Could I be seeing things? I resisted the urge to tug off my goggles. More darkened shapes appeared around us. Pax's head was down as he continued forward. He hadn't seen what I saw—pine trees. We couldn't be at the base of the mountain yet. My mind went back to the natural landmarks of the mountain I saw from the Main Lodge, the lines Dad traced from our den window, and the line I'd plotted from the summit. I knew where we were at, which meant one thing.

I summoned all my energy and ran to cut off Pax before he walked right off the cliff. "Pax, stop!" My feet were heavy with fatigue, like they were cement blocks. Pax didn't lift his head. "Pax!" I called again and reached for his jacket sleeve. He stopped as I slid in front of him, my snowboard swinging a large arc across the snow. I could feel the weight of it as it skidded over the edge of the cliff and that was enough to knock me off balance. The snowboard leash attached to my leg snapped and pulled me back a step. One second I stood before my brother, and the next, I was falling.

CHAPTER 18

A strangled gasp caught in my throat as the ground disappeared from under me. The sensation of free fall took hold of my stomach and squeezed. *Can this really be happening?* It was as if the moment was playing out in slow motion, yet I couldn't do anything about it.

"Jessa!" Pax screamed and reached out for me. His arms looped around me, but I slipped through.

Frantically, I clawed the air as I fell. "Pax!" I cried. My hand swung out in one final attempt to grab the ledge before it was all over. This time gravity was on my side. I missed the rocky lip of the cliff, but my hand managed to hook my brother's ankle. The jolt of my weight knocked him off his feet, and he hit the snow hard with a grunt. I came to a sudden stop and the momentum slammed me into the mountain wall. I groaned as pain radiated down my side, but I kept my hands wrapped around Pax's ankle.

"Hold on," Pax called above me, his voice strained.

"Trust me, I'm not letting go." I clung to his leg. My already numb fingers ached to keep their grip. Pax pulled me up a few inches so my eye line was now at cliff level. He used his free foot to brace himself against the uneven terrain of the mountain where rocks jutted out of the snow. His right armed hooked another protruding rock like an anchor.

"Give me your hand." Pax stretched out his left arm, his face scrunched in pain, and grabbed my wrist.

I released his leg with one hand and wrapped it around his wrist. "Don't lct me go." Tears stung my eyes.

Pax tried to tug me back over the edge but

my snowboard leash wouldn't budge, keeping half of me dangling over the edge. The rocky ledge dug into my stomach. "I've got you, Jess," he said reassuringly.

"I'm caught." I tried to pull my leg up to swing it over the cliff, but the leash kept me right where I was. "I think it's my board."

"I don't know if I can hold you much longer." Pax strained against my weight and his hold on the mountain.

I glanced at my feet. The wind whipped my braid from side to side and scattered the snow around me. A thick root or branch jutted out from the mountainside like an arm, and in its clutches was my board. *What do I do?* Solutions flooded my mind.

"It's tangled. I think I can free it," I called over the roar of the wind.

"What? No, Jessa, I'm slipping," Pax pleaded.

"Just give me a second." I wedged my free foot in a notch on the underside of the cliff for leverage and to relieve Pax of some of my weight. My leash was just hooked on a tiny branch. I could swing my leg and free it.

"Jessa, stop!" he yelled.

I swung my leg and the leash scooted across the branch an inch. *I can do this*, I thought. I wasn't losing my new board, not after I'd come this far.

"Jessa, for once listen to me," Pax demanded.

I tried again and the leash moved a half inch more. *Almost there.*

"Jessa, please, I can't hold you. Let it go," Pax said.

"Let it go?" I looked up at him. I couldn't be hearing him right. "But I can't, my board—"

Pax shook his head. I could feel his grip slowly losing strength the longer we stayed in this position. I swallowed a sob and nodded back at him. *He's right. I know what I have to do.*

I reached down and released the strap from my leg. The weight of the board unraveled the leash from the branch, and it plummeted into the white nothingness below.

CHAPTER 19

The wind died down after that.

Without the added weight of my board, I was able to swing my leg over the ledge. Pax freed up his other arm and pulled me the rest of the way to safety. I picked myself up off the snowy cliff and helped Pax to his feet. The snow continued to fall, but now it was slow and lazy like feathers drifting down from the sky.

"Are you okay?" I asked.

Pax sniffled. With his goggles on I couldn't tell if he'd been crying. "I'll tell you when we get back to the Main Lodge. Right now, I still can't believe we're alive."

"Yeah, me neither. I'm happy you came

along though. I guess I'll have to thank Dad
for having you babysit me."

"Yeah, sure." Pax's voice cracked.

"And thank you," I said, swallowing back my
own emotion, "for saving my life."

Pax bear hugged me, crushing me into him.
He didn't say another word—just squeezed
me tight until he was ready to let go. We didn't
talk about the cliff again.

The change in snow made the visibility better,
enough for me to make out the downward slope
of the mountain. We still tossed snowballs ahead
of us in case we missed any snowdrift-covered
crevices. Although the worst of the storm had
passed, we were far from home.

"You know what?" Pax asked. With his
arm draped over my shoulder for support, I
helped him down a steep patch of snow. The
cold and the strain of pulling me to safety had
weakened him.

I looked up at him, trying to detect any
signs of concern. "What?"

"I could seriously eat an entire large pizza
right now," he said with a wink.

"Isn't that pretty normal?" I asked, and we both laughed.

* * *

We trekked through the snow for a while before we saw the snowmobiles' headlights. White orbs of light flickered in and out of the pine forest below us. I'd never been more relieved in my life.

"Here, here! We're over here," Pax called and waved his free arm.

Several snowmobiles and a medic came to our rescue with a stretcher in tow. They wrapped my brother in blankets and drove him back to the lodge where paramedics waited to assess him for hypothermia. I followed behind on another snowmobile.

"Your parents are on their way. They got caught in the storm back in town and had to wait it out," the lodge manager said. He seated me by the fire with a cup of cocoa after a medic checked me out.

"How's my brother?" I asked as I took the hot chocolate from him.

"He's still with the paramedics, but as soon as he's cleared I'll bring him over."

I thanked him and snuggled into the large arm chair, the fire warming me. The heat from the mug seeped into my hands, and the sweet scent of chocolate filled my nose. I didn't think I'd ever admit it, but I was relieved to be off the slopes. I brought the mug to my lips and let the hot chocolatey goodness warm me from the inside out.

"Hey, Castillo." Ollie appeared and sat down on the chair closest to me.

"Hey." I rested my mug on my lap, but my hands remained wrapped around it. "I guess you heard."

"Yeah, I was the one who reported you were missing."

"How did you know?" I couldn't stop myself from hoping he'd been waiting for me to finish my run. It was silly—he probably regretted taking me up there after what I'd done.

"You called the ski shop. I could hear you, but you couldn't hear me." Firelight danced across Ollie's face.

"Oh. Then I should be thanking you for saving my life too." I didn't intend for it to come out ungrateful, but I couldn't mask my disappointment. *He only noticed my absence because my distress call went through.*

"I was worried about you." Ollie glanced at the floor and covered the back of his neck with his hand. "When you didn't come back down and stop by the shop"—he looked at me and shrugged—"I thought something might be wrong."

I smiled. *Guess he was waiting for me after all.* "Well, thank you," I responded with a grin. "I guess I owe you for more than just getting me on that lift. We wouldn't have been rescued without you."

"I don't know if I deserve that much credit." Ollie held my gaze, his expression serious. "I heard what you did up there, Jessa. There would've been no one to rescue if you didn't make it as far as you did. You guys were really brave."

He called me Jessa. My cheeks burned hot, and I had a feeling it had nothing to do with the fire or the hot cocoa. "Thanks, but I think I still owe you one."

Ollie smiled. "Yeah, you do."

"It might be a while before I can repay you. I may be grounded for some time after this." *I just hope it's not for life.*

"I can wait." Ollie smiled wider.

I did the same, but it didn't last. "I lost my new board," I sighed.

"Oh, I'm sorry. It was a pretty sweet ride."

"Yeah, well, I guess I can use my old board until I save up for another one," I said. *Even if I'd have to shovel a hundred driveways to get it.*

"I bet I could let you borrow a demo for the competition."

"Really?" I asked, excitedly. It wouldn't be mine, but I'd take it.

"Sure. It shouldn't be a problem, and we can hit the terrain park too. You can show me how you stomp those landings."

"Okay, that'd be great." Then I remembered my punishment and my enthusiasm faded as fast as it had appeared. "We'll have to wait until my dad un-grounds me after what happened today."

Ollie gave me a sympathetic nod. "Maybe until then you can introduce me to your dad."

I raised my eyebrows in surprise.

"Um, I mean, as Ethan 'the Ripper' Castillo. Not like *meeting-meeting* your dad, but meeting the professional snowboarder."

"Right. Okay, you've got a deal." I nodded. "But just the terrain park? I heard the backcountry run is worth the risk. You should know, I don't give up so easily."

About the Author

Vanessa Lanang makes her home in Los Angeles, CA, with her family, an insatiable passion for baking, and a resilient poinsettia plant that has yet to discover Christmas is over. When she isn't writing and drinking copious amounts of coffee, she can be found playing tennis or watching her daughters swim.

TO THE LIMIT

OFF ROAD

ON EDGE

RIPTIDE

WHITEOUT

CHECK OUT ALL THE TITLES IN THE

TO THE LIMIT SERIES

DAY OF DISASTER

Would you survive?